LUNA DESTINY
AND THE
MOON BERETS
IN
THE THREE-LEGGED
SPACE RACE
ZZZZZ
AHH! WHAT A LOVELY AND PEACEFUL MORNING.
ZZZZZ
HEH-HEH!
ZZZZZ
ZZZZZ
AAAHHH!!!
YEOW!
YIEE!
DON'T YOU RUN AWAY FROM ME, YOU LITTLE RASCAL!
AHRRR!
ONE DAY I'LL CATCH YOU!
HA-HA!
SERIOUSLY, WHO IS THAT KID?
LUNA DESTINY, READY FOR ACTION!
?
ZOOM!

OH WELL! I SEE WE ARE ALL AWAKE.
NOW, LET'S GET STARTED
YAWN!
WHY ARE WE UP SO EARLY?
I'M READY! I'M READY! I'M READY!
ON TODAY'S AGENDA IS THE THREE-LEGGED RACE.
THE TEAM THAT BEST USES COOPERATION TO CROSS THE FINISH LINE WILL RECEIVE A NEW VICTORY MOONPIN.
I'LL SEE EVERYONE AT THE STARTING LINE IN FIVE MINUTES.
SHRIEK!
A SHINY NEW MOONPIN!
OOOH... I LOVE COLLECTING PINS SOOO MUCH!
I'LL BE THE SHINIEST MOON BERET WHEN I COLLECT THEM ALL.
BARNABY! WE'D BETTER HURRY UP AND GET A GOOD SPOT AT THE STARTING LINE!
I NEED TO WIN THIS!
I'M PRETTY SURE THIS ISN'T HOW COOPERATION WORKS, LUNA.
OH LOOK, HOW CUTE! LUNA THINKS SHE HAS A CHANCE OF WINNING TODAY.
?
?
GIVE IT UP, LUNA! WEST AND I HAVE BEEN PRACTICING FOR THE THREE-LEGGED RACE ALL WEEK.
THAT VICTORY PIN IS OURS FOR SURE.
HAR-HA!
GRRR!
LET HER GO, LUNA.
MIRANDA IS JUST A MEAN-SPIRITED GIRL.

SHE SURE HAS A BIG MOUTH.
YOU'RE RIGHT, BARNABY. I SHOULDN'T LET HER GET TO ME.
ESPECIALLY WHEN I KNOW WE'RE GUARANTEED TO WIN.
WHAT MAKES YOU SO SURE?
BECAUSE MY NAME IS LUNA...
... AND I ALWAYS HAVE A PLAN.
BEHOLD! THE AIR PLUTO 9000!
FASTEST HIGH-TOP RUNNING SHOE IN THE GALAXY.
HOLD ON A SECOND!
WOULDN'T THIS BE CONSIDERED CHEATING?
UM... MAYBE?
THERE AREN'T RULES AGAINST IT IN THE MOON BERET'S GUIDE BOOK .
SO I SAY, LET'S GIVE IT A TRY!
THE MOON BERET GUIDE BOOK
BUT WAIT!
TRUST ME!
JUST PUT YOUR FOOT IN THE SHOE NEXT TO MINE. LIKE THIS!
FEET SECURED!
IT'S VOICE-ACTIVATED. PRETTY COOL, HUH?
NOW, WHEN WE GET TO THE STARTING LINE, WE JUST SAY THE ULTRA-TOP-SECRET-ACTIVATION CODE,
AND WE'LL BE THE FASTEST THREE-LEGGED TEAM OUT THERE!

HEY, WAIT A MINUTE!
BY ANY CHANCE, IS THIS SO-CALLED TOP SECRET CODE 1-2-3 GO?
1-2-3 GO!
BEEP! BEEP! BEEP!
WHAT'S HAPPENING?!
OH NO! YOU JUST ACTIVATED THE SHOE!
1-2-3 GO!
AIR PLUTO 9000 ACTIVATED!
AAAHHH!!!
DID I MENTION THAT THE SHOE IS PROGRAMMED FOR MAXIMUM SPEED?
AAAAAAAAA
OK TROOPS! ON YOUR MARK, GET SET, ...
I GUESS LUNA GOT COLD FEET. HE-HE!
AAAAAAAAAAA
WATCH OUT! HOT FEET COMING THROUGH!
ZOOOOOM
LUNA! MAKE IT STOP!
I CAN'T! I NEVER FINISHED READING THE INSTRUCTIONS.

AAAAAAAAAAAAAAAAAAAAAAAAAAAAAAA
SPLASH!
?
BUZZZZ
OH NO! I'M TOO YOUNG TO SHAVE.
ME TOO!
SORRY LITTLE FOREST BUDDIES!
BUZZZZZ
THEY ARE SO SOFT ON THE OUTSIDE BUT SO MEAN ON THE INSIDE!
GRRR!!
OH! HI THERE BIG FELLA!
NICE TEDDY BEAR. GOOD TEDDY BEAR.
BUZZZZZZ

NOW I CAN'T SEE ANYTHING!
UH, YOU AREN'T MISSING MUCH.
JUST A HUGE TREE HEADING OUR WAY!!
AAAAAAAAAAAAAAAA
GASP!
ACK!
AIR PLUTO 9000 SLEEP MODE INITIATED!
HEY, LOOK AT THE BRIGHT SIDE. AT LEAST THE SHOE STOPPED.
HE-HE!
AAAH!!!
CRASH!
OK, NOTHING TO BE WORRIED ABOUT, BARN. THIS IS JUST A SMALL SETBACK. WE CAN STILL WIN THIS.
YOUR RECKLESS OPTIMISM IS GIVING ME A TUMMY ACHE.

NOW, LET ME SEE HERE.
IF WE TAKE A SHORTCUT WE CAN STILL CATCH UP AND BEAT THAT SASS MOUTHED MIRANDA TO THE FINISH LINE.
ARRG!
SHOULDN'T WE WORRY ABOUT GETTING OUR FEET UNSTUCK FIRST?
BUT FIRST WE NEED TO GET OUR FEET UNSTUCK.
GEE, REALLY! I ALREADY TRIED THAT.
GRUNT!
CURSE MY CUTE LITTLE ARMS! I CAN ALMOST REACH THE BRANCH.
I ALMOST...
WAIT, LET ME TRY TO REACH THE TREE TRUNK FIRST.
ACK!
I ALMOST...
TOK!
OUCH!
THAT'S SOME THICK SKULL YOU HAVE, BARNABY.
ARE YOU OK?
MY HEAD IS FINE, BUT MY TEAM SPIRIT IS A LITTLE BRUISED.
CHIN UP, BUDDY.
WE'LL FIND A WAY OUT OF THIS LIKE WE ALWAYS DO.
AS A TEAM!
WELL, TEAM-MATE, YOU BETTER START THINKING FAST.
TODAY IS HOT CHOCO-LOCO TUESDAY AND SCOUTMASTER PILAR ALWAYS GIVES AWAY EXTRA MARSHMALLOWS TO THE FIRST TEAM TO FINISH.
AND I LOVES ME SOME EXTRA MALLOWS IN MY BELLY.

THINK, LUNA, THINK!
YOU ARE GOOD AT THIS.
USE THAT NOGGIN GIRL!
WHAT IF WE PUSH AGAINST THE TREE, AND SWING UP TO GRAB THE BOOT?
HEY, I GOT IT! LET'S SWING TO THAT SIDE OF THE TREE, AND PUSH OURSELVES UP TO GRAB THE SHOE!
WAIT! THAT'S WHAT I...
SIGH!
OK, LET'S DO IT TOGETHER ON THE COUNT OF THREE. ONE, TWO, THREE...
NO, WAIT!!!
SLAP!
GO!
AIR PLUTO 9000 ACTIVATED!
BEEP! BEEP! BEEP!
RATTLE!
AH-RR-R!
GR-RR-RR!!
POP!
HEY BARN, CAN YOU WIGGLE YOUR TOES FREELY?
YES. WHY?
OH, NOTHING. JUST CHECKING.
AAAAAAA
DROP
AAAAAAA

HUFF!
ACK!
FLOP
HEY! WE'RE *FREE!* WHAT DID I TELL YOU? OUR PLAN *WORKED.*
I'M *CONFUSED.* WHEN WAS *FALLING* TO THE GROUND PART OF THE PLAN?
OUCH! MY FOOT *HURTS!*
YIKES! MY FOOT IS SORE *TOO.*
OH NO! MY TOES ARE *THROBBING* IN PAIN!
WAAAH!!!
NOW WE'RE NEVER GETTING BACK TO CAMP!
DON'T *CRY*, BARN. THIS IS ALL MY *FAULT*, I'LL GET YOU BACK TO CAMP. I PROMISE.
WAIT A MINUTE! I THINK I'VE GOT AN *IDEA!*
FIRST, LET'S TAKE OUR *SOCKS* OFF...
POP!
SOB!
... AND THEN TIE THEM TOGETHER AROUND OUR INJURED FEET.

NOW WE CAN HELP EACH OTHER WALK!
SEE! WITH A LITTLE COOPERATION WE'LL GET BACK TO CAMP IN NO TIME!
NOW YOU GET IT!
CHECK US OUT! WE'RE PRETTY GOOD AT THIS.
HEY, THIS IS FUN!
GASP! GO ON WITHOUT ME.
HUFF! I'M TRYING.
STOP PULLING!
NO! YOU STOP PULLING!
WE DID IT, LUNA! WE WON THE THREE-LEGGED RACE!
AND THE VICTORY PIN TOO!
?
!
ZZZZ
WHAT DID I TELL YOU LUNA? TEAMWORK ALWAYS PAYS OFF.
YES IT DOES. IT PAYS WITH A SHINY NEW PIN AND ALL THE HOT CHOCOLATE WE CAN DRINK!
WINK!
THE END

HIP AND POPO
IN TWO HEADS ARE BETTER THAN ONE
HIP MY MAN, YOU MAKE THE BEST MANGO SMOOTHIES IN THE ENTIRE GALAXY!
THANKS, POPO! MANGO SMOOTHIES ARE MY JAM. MY SECRET INGREDIENT IS MANGOS.
MAN! THE WATER IS MUCH WARMER THAN I EXPECTED.
REALLY? I DIDN'T NOTICE.
SIIIP!
OH, BEEPING BUBBLES! I KNOW WHAT THAT MEANS!
YOU KNOW IT, BUDDY, WE'RE BEING SUMMONED TO THE COMMAND CENTER!
BEEP!
BEEP!
BEEP!
WAIT! MAKE SURE THE COAST IS CLEAR. WE DON'T WANT ANYONE SPYING ON US.
SPYING? LIKE THAT ARMY GUY WHO IS ALWAYS TRYING TO STEAL ALL YOUR SPACE ALIEN SECRETS, AND WHO IS HIDING BEHIND THOSE GIANT FERNS?
YOU KNOW. THE DUDE WITH THE UGLY MUSTACHE?
HEY! WHAT'S WRONG WITH MY "STACHE"? EVERYONE KNOWS THAT MUSTACHES ARE IN THESE DAYS.

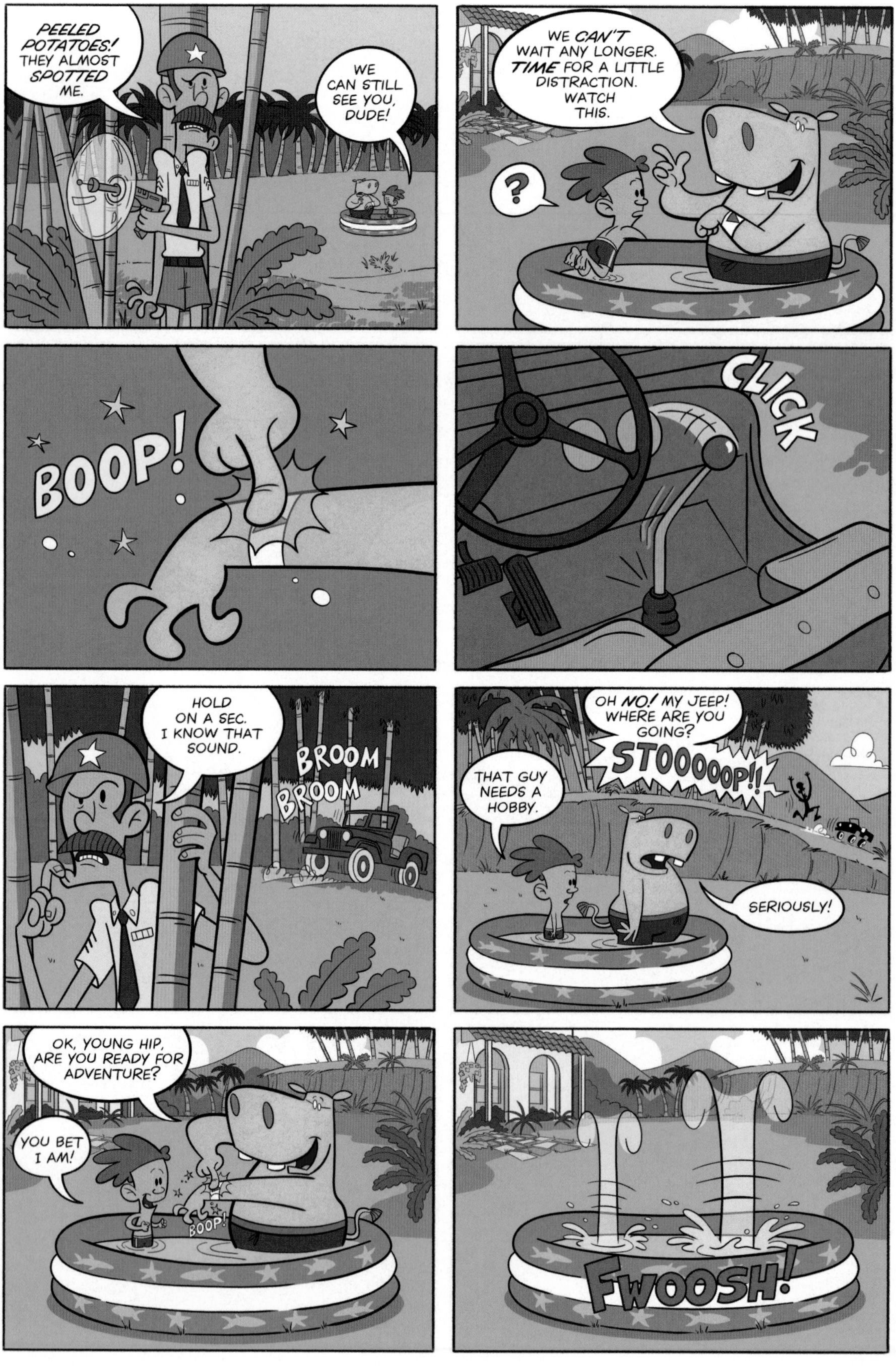
PEELED POTATOES! THEY ALMOST SPOTTED ME.
WE CAN STILL SEE YOU, DUDE!
WE CAN'T WAIT ANY LONGER. TIME FOR A LITTLE DISTRACTION. WATCH THIS.
?
BOOP!
CLICK
HOLD ON A SEC. I KNOW THAT SOUND.
BROOM
BROOM
OH NO! MY JEEP! WHERE ARE YOU GOING?
STOOOOOP!!
THAT GUY NEEDS A HOBBY.
SERIOUSLY!
OK, YOUNG HIP, ARE YOU READY FOR ADVENTURE?
YOU BET I AM!
BOOP!
FWOOSH!

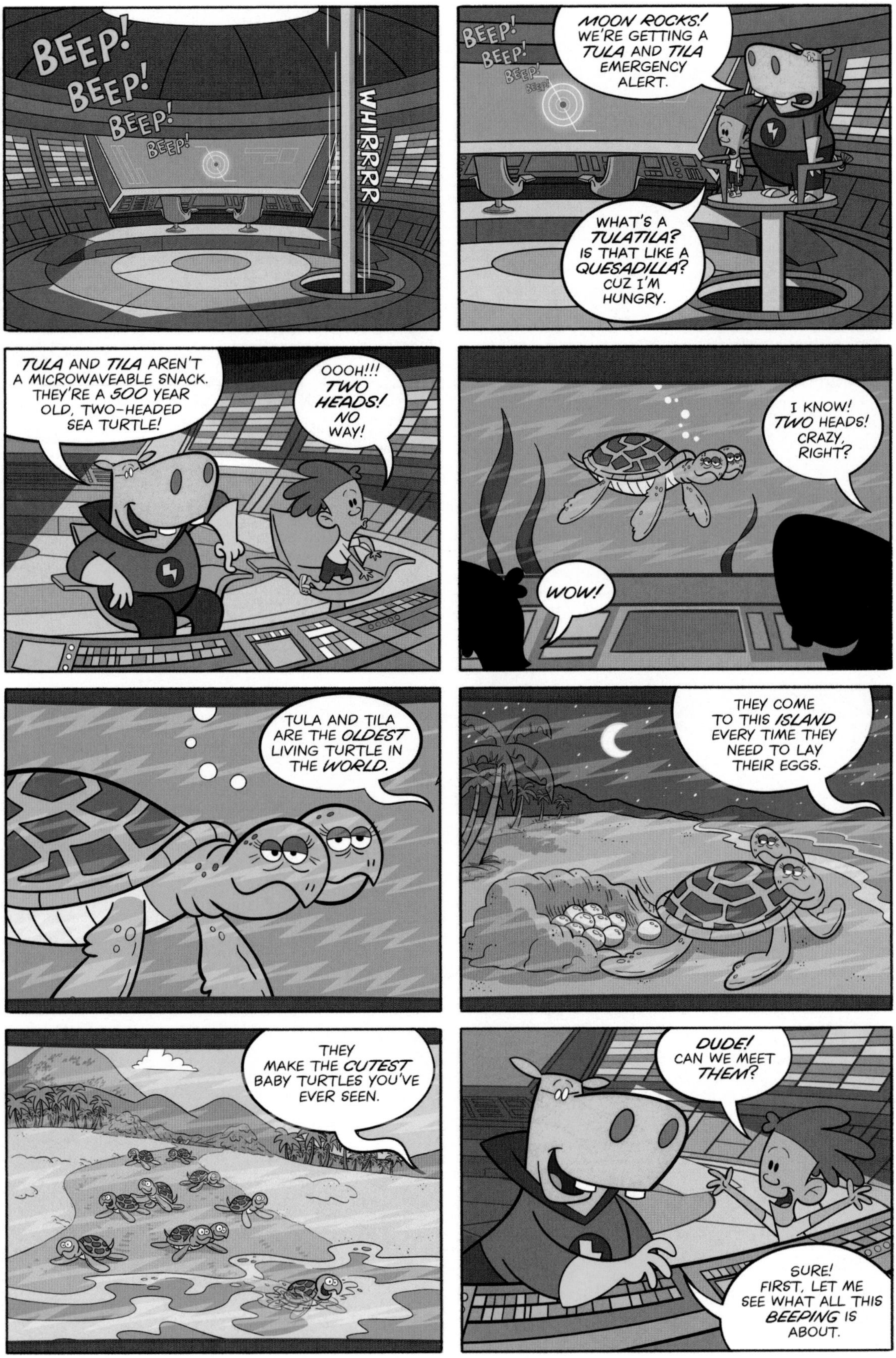
BEEP! BEEP! BEEP! BEEP!
WHIRRRR
BEEP! BEEP! BEEP! BEEP!
MOON ROCKS! WE'RE GETTING A TULA AND TILA EMERGENCY ALERT.
WHAT'S A TULATILA? IS THAT LIKE A QUESADILLA? CUZ I'M HUNGRY.
TULA AND TILA AREN'T A MICROWAVEABLE SNACK. THEY'RE A 500 YEAR OLD, TWO-HEADED SEA TURTLE!
OOOH!!! TWO HEADS! NO WAY!
I KNOW! TWO HEADS! CRAZY, RIGHT?
WOW!
TULA AND TILA ARE THE OLDEST LIVING TURTLE IN THE WORLD.
THEY COME TO THIS ISLAND EVERY TIME THEY NEED TO LAY THEIR EGGS.
THEY MAKE THE CUTEST BABY TURTLES YOU'VE EVER SEEN.
DUDE! CAN WE MEET THEM?
SURE! FIRST, LET ME SEE WHAT ALL THIS BEEPING IS ABOUT.

OH NO! THERE IS SOMETHING WRONG!
WHAT?
THEY'RE SWIMMING IN CIRCLES. THEY MUST BE IN TROUBLE.
HURRY! WE HAVE TO HELP THEM GET TO THE BEACH SO THEY CAN LAY THEIR EGGS!!!
YOU'RE RIGHT, HIP! THEY DO NEED OUR HELP!
ALRIGHT!
BUT FIRST, WE NEED SOME EQUIPMENT.
EQUIPMENT?
BOOP!
ZZZING!!!
SURFBOARDS! NICE THINKING, DUDE.
I ALWAYS LIKE TO GO ON A RESCUE MISSION IN STYLE.
TOTALLY!
SEATBELT ON! LETS GO!!!
WOOHOOOO!!!
WHOOSH!

GRUMBLE GRUMBLE.
THIS IS THE LAST TIME I LET THOSE TWO JOKESTERS MAKE A FOOL OF ME.
SERIOUSLY, WHAT RESPONSIBLE PARENT WOULD LET A KID KEEP A ONE-TON HIPPOPOTAMUS FOR A PET?
ZOOM!
IF I COULD ONLY PROVE THAT HE'S AN ALIEN... WAIT! WAS THAT A...
U.F.O.?
CRASH!
KI-KI-RI-KI!
I HATE EVERYTHING.
UH-OH.
BROOM
BROOM
click!
NOT AGAIN! PLEASE STOOOOP!!!
SOMETIMES I CAN'T HELP MYSELF.
SHENANIGANS!

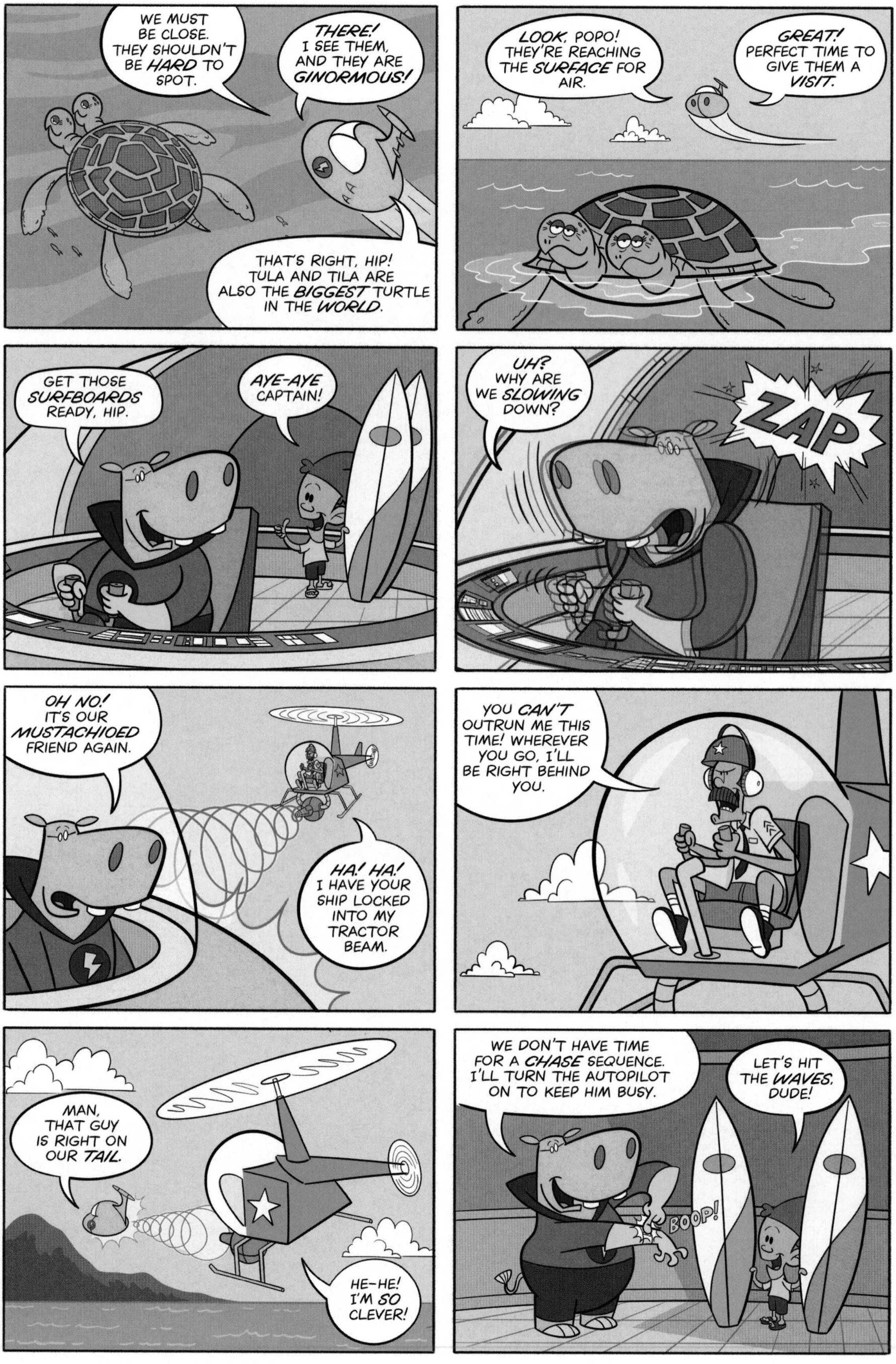
WE MUST BE CLOSE. THEY SHOULDN'T BE HARD TO SPOT.
THERE! I SEE THEM, AND THEY ARE GINORMOUS!
THAT'S RIGHT, HIP! TULA AND TILA ARE ALSO THE BIGGEST TURTLE IN THE WORLD.
LOOK, POPO! THEY'RE REACHING THE SURFACE FOR AIR.
GREAT! PERFECT TIME TO GIVE THEM A VISIT.
GET THOSE SURFBOARDS READY, HIP.
AYE-AYE CAPTAIN!
UH? WHY ARE WE SLOWING DOWN?
ZAP
OH NO! IT'S OUR MUSTACHIOED FRIEND AGAIN.
HA! HA! I HAVE YOUR SHIP LOCKED INTO MY TRACTOR BEAM.
YOU CAN'T OUTRUN ME THIS TIME! WHEREVER YOU GO, I'LL BE RIGHT BEHIND YOU.
MAN, THAT GUY IS RIGHT ON OUR TAIL.
HE-HE! I'M SO CLEVER!
WE DON'T HAVE TIME FOR A CHASE SEQUENCE. I'LL TURN THE AUTOPILOT ON TO KEEP HIM BUSY.
BOOP!
LET'S HIT THE WAVES, DUDE!

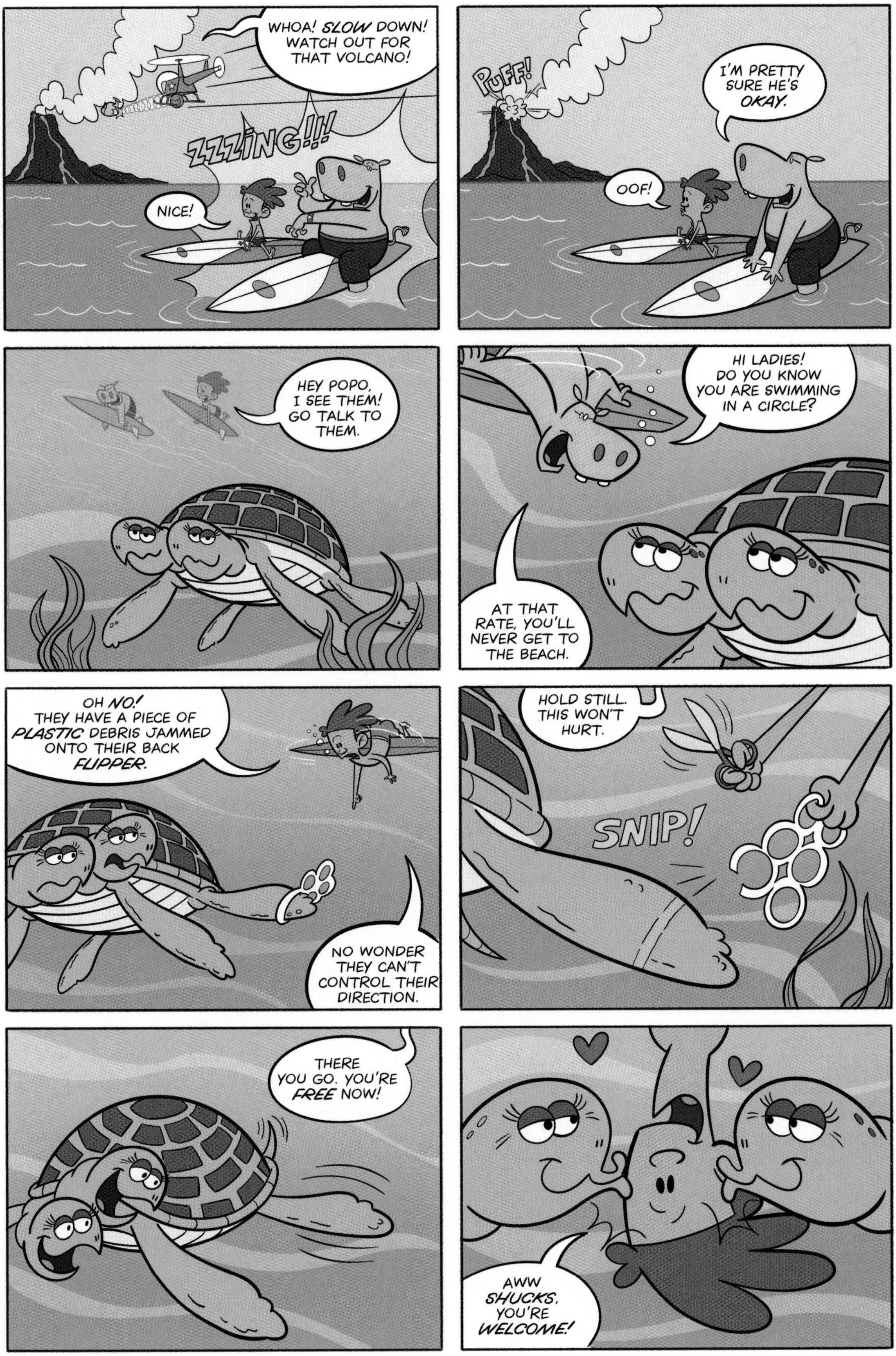
WHOA! SLOW DOWN! WATCH OUT FOR THAT VOLCANO!
ZZZING!!!
NICE!
PUFF!
I'M PRETTY SURE HE'S OKAY.
OOF!
HEY POPO, I SEE THEM! GO TALK TO THEM.
HI LADIES! DO YOU KNOW YOU ARE SWIMMING IN A CIRCLE?
AT THAT RATE, YOU'LL NEVER GET TO THE BEACH.
OH NO! THEY HAVE A PIECE OF PLASTIC DEBRIS JAMMED ONTO THEIR BACK FLIPPER.
NO WONDER THEY CAN'T CONTROL THEIR DIRECTION.
HOLD STILL. THIS WON'T HURT.
SNIP!
THERE YOU GO. YOU'RE FREE NOW!
AWW SHUCKS, YOU'RE WELCOME!

I THINK THEY LIKE ME.
NO TIME FOR ROMANCE! IT'S EGG LAYING TIME!
HEY HIP, LET'S ESCORT THESE LOVELY LADIES TO THE BEACH.
IT'S MY PLEASURE!
THE BEACH IS STRAIGHT AHEAD.
LET'S PADDLE!
HEY GUYS, CHECK OUT THAT WAVE! WE CAN'T PASS ON THIS SWEET RIDE.
WOW! LOOK AT THEM. FOR A QUINCENTENARIAN, THEY SURE HAVE SOME COOL MOVES.
WOOHoo!
LOOK HOW HAPPY TULA AND TILA ARE!
THAT WAS FUN!
HEH-HEH!

LOOK AT THEM DIG A NEST ON THE SAND!
OH! I THINK WE SHOULD LET THE GIRLS HAVE SOME PRIVACY, HIP.
POPO, LOOK!!!
MORE TURTLES!
THOUSANDS OF THEM.
THAT'S RIGHT, HIP, TULA AND TILA AREN'T THE ONLY ONES THAT COME TO THIS ISLAND TO LAY THEIR EGGS.
SOME OF THEM MIGHT EVEN BE HER GRANDCHILDREN.
WOW!
YOU THINK SHE WILL LET ME NAME THE BABIES?
I'LL GIVE THEM COOL NAMES LIKE, SHELL SHOCK, SNAPPY JACKIE, SWIFTY MCQUEEN, AND DAVE.
HA-HA! YOU DON'T HAVE TO NAME THEM ALL RIGHT AWAY. IT'LL TAKE A COUPLE OF MONTHS FOR THE EGGS TO HATCH.
GOOD, BECAUSE IT'S GOING TO BE A LONG LIST. HA-HA!
WHAT IS SO FUNNY, GENTLEMEN?

ONE SUDDEN MOVE AND I'LL USE THIS NET CANNON ON THE TWO OF YOU.
HA-HA! THERE IS NO WAY YOU CAN ESCAPE ME THIS TIME.
WOW! WHAT HAPPENED TO YOU?
IF YOU'RE TRYING TO MAKE A FASHION STATEMENT, IT'S NOT WORKING.
SHOOSH! QUIET WHILE I'M ON THE PHONE.
HELLO! YES! I HAVE SOMETHING VERY IMPORTANT TO TELL THE GENERAL. ... WHAT? NO, WAIT! DON'T PUT ME ON HOLD!
HEY, POPO. LOOK DOWN! HE-HE!
HA!
WHY ARE YOU TWO BEACH BUMS GIGGLING?
LUMPY POTATOES!!!
BOOM!
RUMLE!
OH NO!
THWAP!
HE-HE!
HE-HE!
I'LL BE BACK!!!
EIGHTEEN IN ONE DAY? CERTAINLY!!!
POPO, WHAT DO YOU SAY TO ANOTHER ROUND OF SMOOTHIES?
THE END

SHERIFF RATTATAN AND DEPUTY PANCHO
IN NO NACHO LEFT BEHIND
RITA'S CANTINA
GREAT PRACTICE TODAY, TEAM! WHO WANTS TO GO TO RITA'S FOR LUNCH?
I DO!
ME TOO!
OH, HAROLD, RITA'S FOR OUR ANNIVERSARY! HOW SWEET OF YOU.
BABE, NOTHING BUT THE BEST FOR YOU!
YUM-YUM!
MAN, RITA'S FOOD IS THE BOMB!
PICK UP
OOOH! MY NUMBER IS NEXT!
MOOO!
I'M SO EXCITED! HEH-HEH!
WAIT HERE
NUMBER 18! TWO ATOMIC TACOS WITH EXTRA BEANS! PICK-UP!
ONE MORE JALAPENO. NICE AND STEADY.
RITA'S FOOD ALWAYS BLOWS ME AWAY.

THERE! AS THE ONLY ELECTED OFFICIAL DINING IN THIS FINE ESTABLISHMENT, I DECLARE YOU A NATIONAL TREASURE.
I ♥ Nach
YES SIR! YOU MIGHT BE THE LAST NACHO ON MY PLATE, BUT YOU SURE ARE THE PRETTIEST!
NOW LET'S CONCLUDE THESE CELEBRATIONS WITH SOME HOT TOMATILLO SAUCE.
HUMPH! WHAT IS THIS? EMPTY!
HUH?
PARDON ME, YOUNG MAN. GOVERNMENT BUSINESS.
I ♥ Nachos
OH NO! SEÑOR NACHO CON QUESO Y FRIJOLES! WHERE HAVE YOU GONE?!
I ♥ Nachos
THIS IS AN OUTRAGE! SOMEONE HAS TAKEN MY LAST NACHO!
I'M YOUR MAYOR AND I DEMAND JUSTICE!
I ♥ Nachos
DID SOMEONE ORDER JUSTICE?!
Rita's
JUSTICE SOUNDS OK, BUT I WAS THINKING OF WAFFLES.

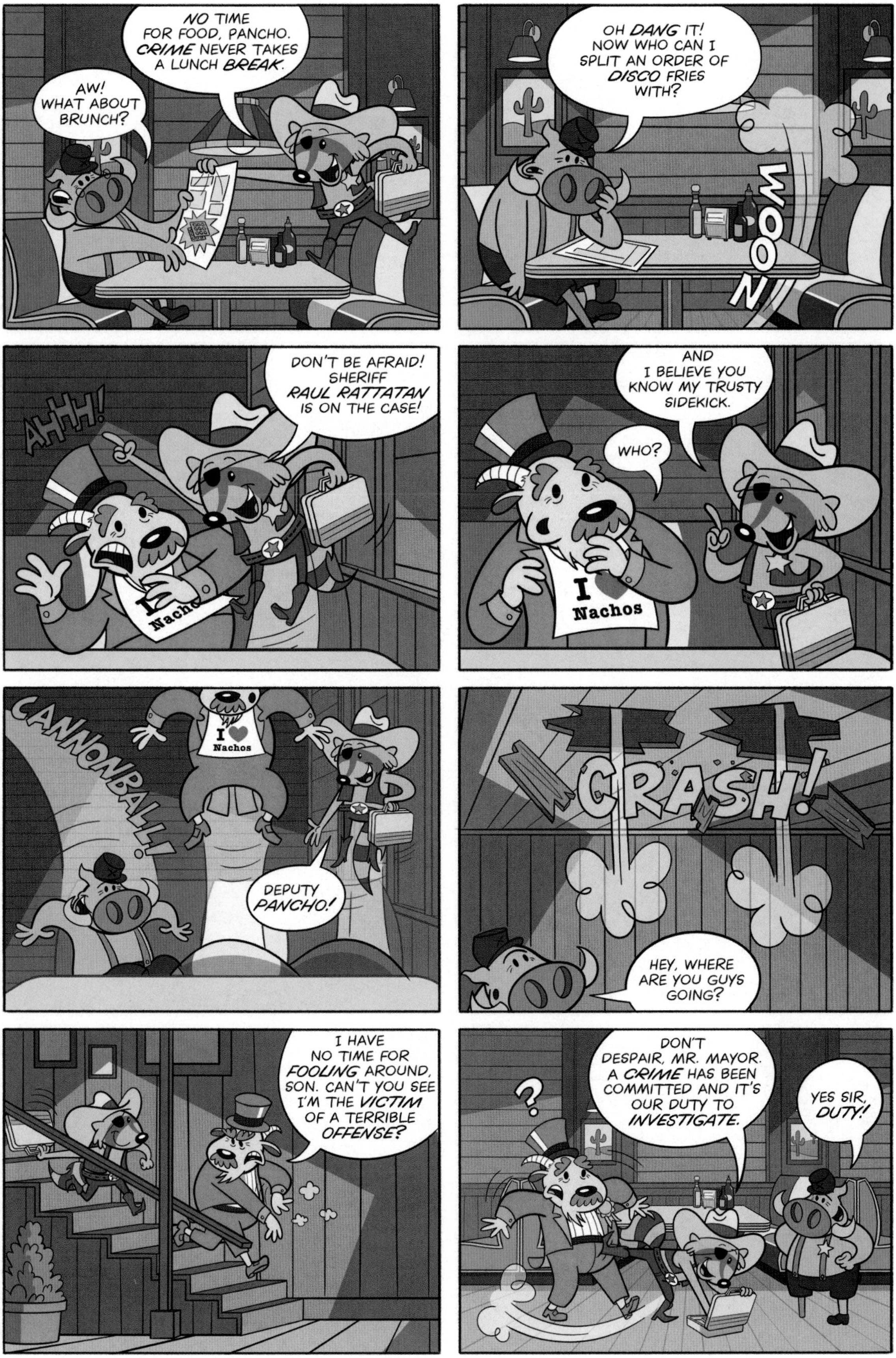
AW! WHAT ABOUT BRUNCH?
NO TIME FOR FOOD, PANCHO. CRIME NEVER TAKES A LUNCH BREAK.
OH DANG IT! NOW WHO CAN I SPLIT AN ORDER OF DISCO FRIES WITH?
WOOOM
AHHH!
DON'T BE AFRAID! SHERIFF RAUL RATTATAN IS ON THE CASE!
I ♥ Nachos
AND I BELIEVE YOU KNOW MY TRUSTY SIDEKICK.
WHO?
I ♥ Nachos
CANNONBALL!
I ♥ Nachos
DEPUTY PANCHO!
CRASH!
HEY, WHERE ARE YOU GUYS GOING?
I HAVE NO TIME FOR FOOLING AROUND, SON. CAN'T YOU SEE I'M THE VICTIM OF A TERRIBLE OFFENSE?
?
DON'T DESPAIR, MR. MAYOR. A CRIME HAS BEEN COMMITTED AND IT'S OUR DUTY TO INVESTIGATE.
YES SIR, DUTY!

OK, MR. MAYOR. FROM THE TOP, DESCRIBE WHAT HAPPENED.
SIGH! VERY WELL.
I WAS OFF THE CAMPAIGNING TRAIL, ENJOYING A DELICIOUS ORDER OF NACHOS.
I MOMENTARILY TURNED MY BACK TO GRAB A BOTTLE OF HOT SAUCE.
AND WHEN I TURNED AROUND, MY LAST NACHO WAS GONE. GONE!
OH NO! A SNACK-JACKING! THIS IS SERIOUS, MR. MAYOR.
THAT MEANS THE KIDNAPPER COULD STILL BE IN THIS ROOM!
A NACHO BANDIT HIDING AT THIS RESTAURANT, HM?
BUT WHO WOULD BE FOOLHARDY ENOUGH TO CHASE AFTER SOMEONE SO DESPICABLE?
AHEM! I BELIEVE YOU ARE HOLDING THAT FOOL.
HE SURE IS!
ALRIGHT, BUT IF YOU TWO DON'T FIND MY LAST NACHO BEFORE MY LUNCH BREAK IS OVER...
YES?
I SHALL REFUSE TO LEAVE A TIP!
GASP!
NO TIP!
NO TIP!
NO TIP!
NO TIP!
CRASH!
OH NO!!! SHERIFF, YOU MUST SOLVE THIS CASE! WE NEED THE MONEY FROM THE TIP JAR TO FIX THE MECHANICAL BULL!
TIPS$

HEY! DOES THIS DARN THING WORK?
TAP! TAP!
SPLAT!
UPH! CAN I GET MY QUARTER BACK?
DON'T YOU WORRY, MISS RITA. PANCHO AND I WILL CAPTURE THIS MYSTERIOUS NACHO-SNATCHER, AND YOU WILL HAVE MONEY IN THAT TIP JAR IN NO TIME.
TIPS
AND THAT IS A SHERIFF PROMISE!
OH RAUL, YOU ARE THE SWEETEST AND BRAVEST LAWMAN IN THE WILD WEST.
ENOUGH COURTSHIP, BACK TO WORK.
NUMBER 22! ONE THUNDER BLASTER BURRITO, WITH A BUCKET OF BEANS. PICK-UP!
SHOVE!
STEP BACK, MR. MAYOR, WE HAVE A CRIME TO SOLVE....
AHH! NOTHING BETTER THAN THE FRESH SMELL OF A NEW CASE.
AHEM!

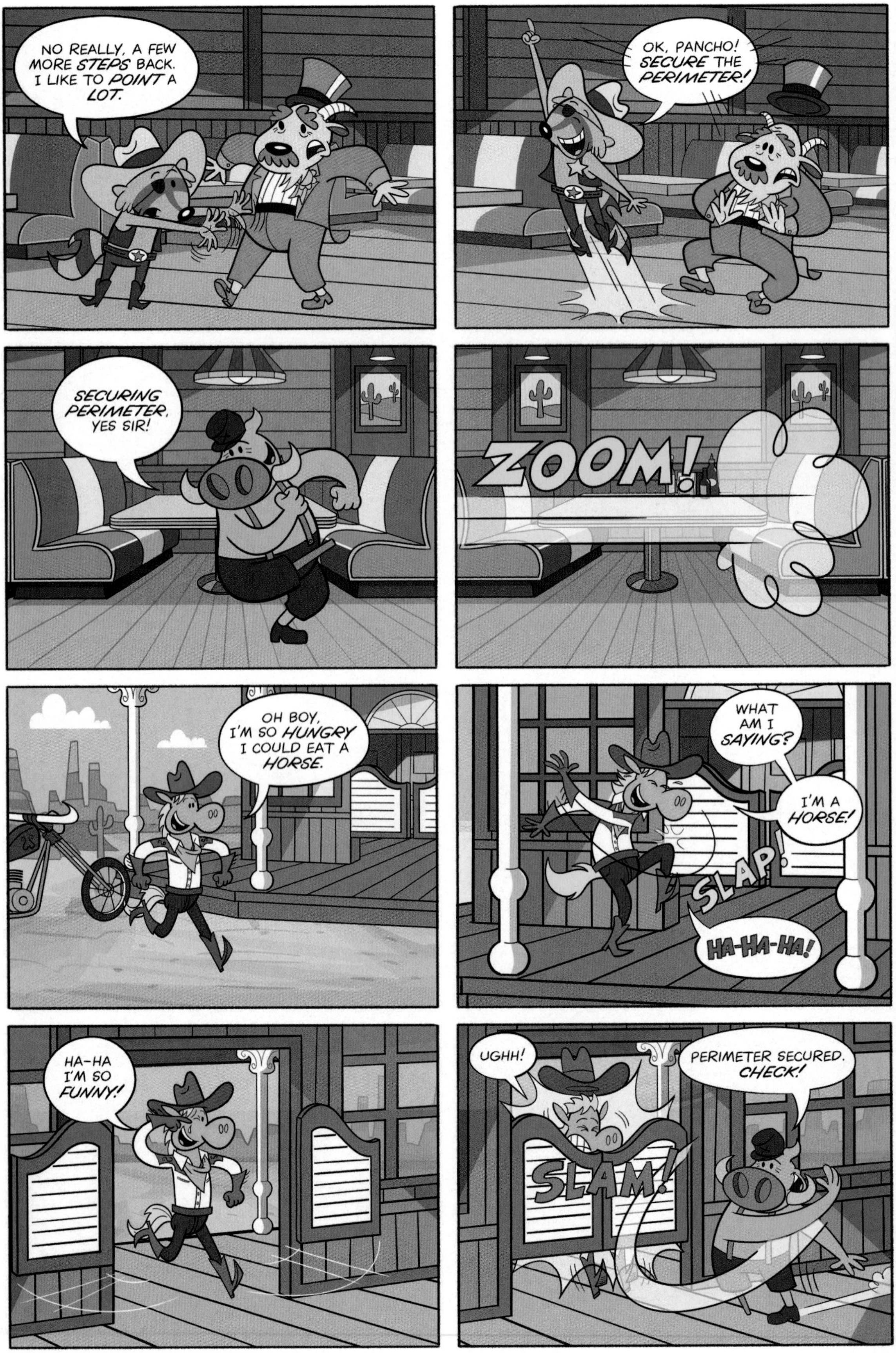
NO REALLY, A FEW MORE STEPS BACK. I LIKE TO POINT A LOT.
OK, PANCHO! SECURE THE PERIMETER!
SECURING PERIMETER, YES SIR!
ZOOM!
OH BOY, I'M SO HUNGRY I COULD EAT A HORSE.
WHAT AM I SAYING?
I'M A HORSE!
SLAP!
HA-HA-HA!
HA-HA I'M SO FUNNY!
UGHH!
PERIMETER SECURED. CHECK!
SLAM!

NEXT STEP: INTERVIEW WITNESSES.
HOWDY AND WELCOME!
WHERE ARE YOU FOLKS FROM?
WE ARE SHERYL AND GREG FROM DULUTH MINNESOTA. ARE WE ON TV?
GREAT! HAVE YOU WITNESSED ANY CRIMES TODAY?
YES! THESE PRICES! ALL YOU CAN EAT BANANA SPLITS. IT'S A STEAL!
WOOHOO! ICE CREAM!!!
CAN I SAY HI TO MY MOM?
HI, MOM!
GRRR! LET GO!
HUMPH! THANK YOU,
ENJOY YOUR MEAL AND DON'T FORGET TO TIP YOUR WAITRESS.
BACK TO YOU, PANCHO.
ACK!
NEXT STEP: PICK UP AND LICK THE EVIDENCE.
YUM!
WHOA! CLOSE ENOUGH, PANCHO.
IT'S "COLLECT AND EXAMINE" THE EVIDENCE."
LET ME SEE HERE.
YES SIR. THAT'S WHAT I MEANT.

AHA! MY TRUSTY SNACK LIGHT!
WITH IT WE CAN VIEW THE GHOST SHAPE OF THE STOLEN NACHO.
LIGHTS, PLEASE!
THIS NACHO WAS MISSING A SHARP CORNER.
WHEN WE FIND THE MISSING NACHO, WE CAN MAKE A COMPARISON AND PROCEED--
WHOA! HOLD ON A SECOND. PANCHO, WHAT IS THAT?
WHAT? DO I HAVE SOMETHING ON MY SNOUT?
BUDDY! I THINK YOU SHOULD CUT DOWN ON THE DONUTS.
NO WAY! DONUTS ARE THE MOST IMPORTANT PART OF A BALANCED BREAKFAST.
YOU MUST BE THINKING OF A HIGH FIBER, MULTI-GRAIN CEREAL.
NO, I'M PRETTY SURE I WAS THINKING ABOUT DONUTS.
CAN YOU GUYS HURRY UP?! WHERE IS MY NACHO?
RIGHT, MR. MAYOR! NEXT... SURVEILLANCE!
SURVEILLANCE WHAT?
ZOOM

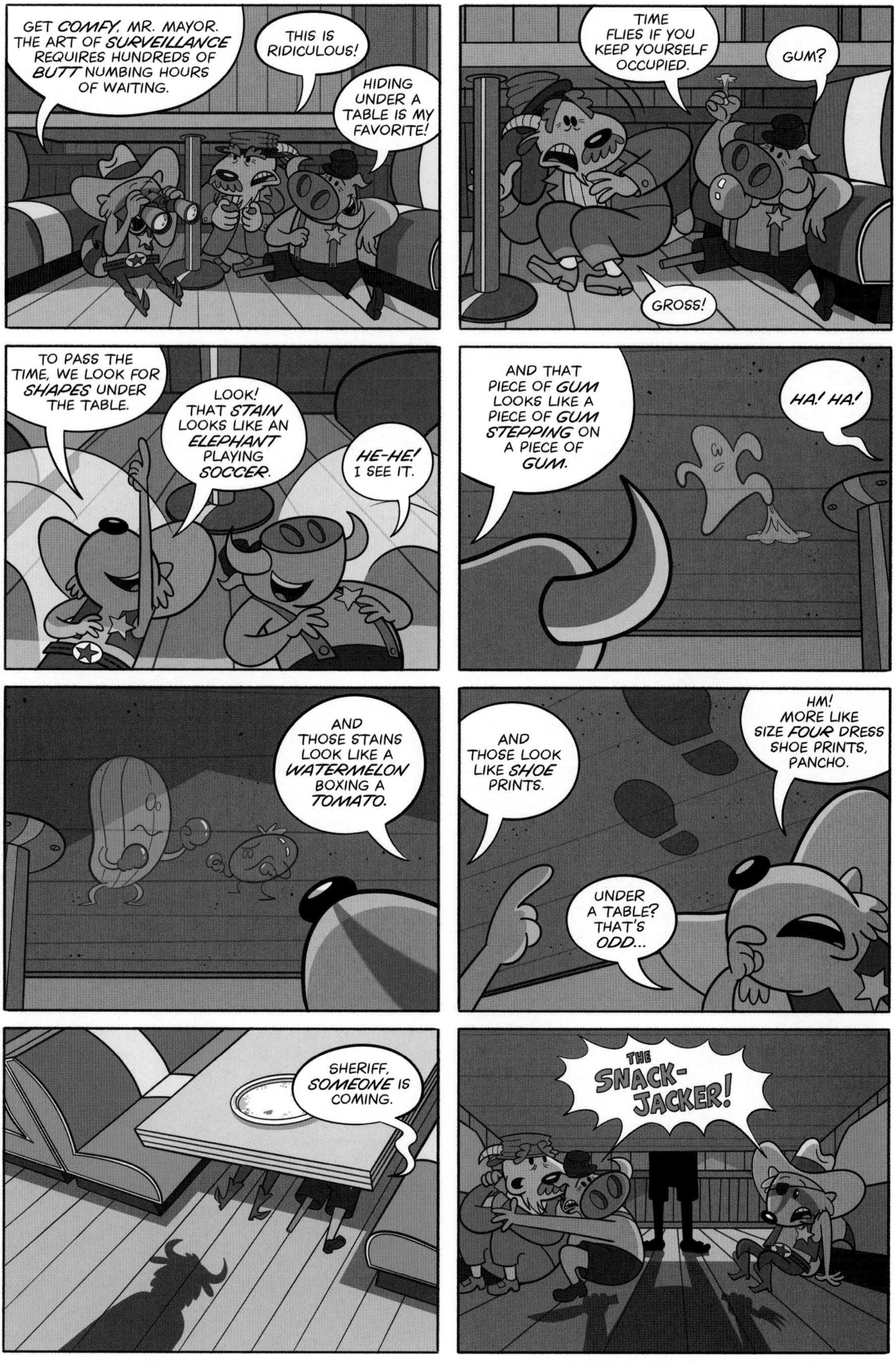
GET COMFY, MR. MAYOR. THE ART OF SURVEILLANCE REQUIRES HUNDREDS OF BUTT NUMBING HOURS OF WAITING.
THIS IS RIDICULOUS!
HIDING UNDER A TABLE IS MY FAVORITE!
TIME FLIES IF YOU KEEP YOURSELF OCCUPIED.
GUM?
GROSS!
TO PASS THE TIME, WE LOOK FOR SHAPES UNDER THE TABLE.
LOOK! THAT STAIN LOOKS LIKE AN ELEPHANT PLAYING SOCCER.
HE-HE! I SEE IT.
AND THAT PIECE OF GUM LOOKS LIKE A PIECE OF GUM STEPPING ON A PIECE OF GUM.
HA! HA!
AND THOSE STAINS LOOK LIKE A WATERMELON BOXING A TOMATO.
AND THOSE LOOK LIKE SHOE PRINTS.
HM! MORE LIKE SIZE FOUR DRESS SHOE PRINTS, PANCHO.
UNDER A TABLE? THAT'S ODD...
SHERIFF, SOMEONE IS COMING.
THE SNACK-JACKER!

JUSTICE GO!
AHHH!
FREEZE! WE HAVE YOU SURROUNDED.
WOW BRO! YOU, LIKE, SCARED ME AND STUFF.
WE ARE LOOKING FOR A SNACK-JACKER, AND YOU FIT THE PROFILE.
I DO?
PANCHO, SKETCH!
I'M ON IT, SHERIFF!
NICE ONE, PANCHO!
THANK YOU, SHERIFF!
YOU KNOW, I WAS A NUDE MODEL BACK IN THE ARMY.
YES SIR. NAKED!
DO YOU KNOW WHAT THIS IS?
SURE, DUDE. THAT'S THE NACHO GRANDE SUPREMO PLATTER.
BIG HIT WITH THE KIDS.
?
AHA! SO YOU ADMIT TO KNOWING IT!
HURRY, PANCHO, TO THE LINEUP.

FOLLOW ME THIS WAY, MR. MAYOR.
DID YOU FIND MY NACHO YET?
ALRIGHT, MR. MAYOR. TAKE YOUR TIME.
DO YOU RECOGNIZE ANYONE IN THIS LINEUP?
HUH?
DON'T BE NERVOUS, THEY DON'T KNOW WE ARE HERE.
I CAN HEAR YOU, BRO.
1
2
3
VERY WELL. I RECKON I RECOGNIZE NUMBER TWO, EDDY.
CONSIDERING THAT HE IS MY NEPHEW AND ALL.
HMM?
HI, UNCLE!
ARE YOU SURE?
NOW THAT I'M LOOKING AT ALL OF THEM, THE GUY ON THE LEFT SEEMS A BIT SKETCHY.
GET OFF ME! OF COURSE I'M SURE!
I KNOW MY OWN KIN WHEN I SEE THEM.
THAT RIGHT THERE IS MY NEPHEW EDDY.
HE IS ALSO MY RIDE HOME TONIGHT.
HOT DIGGITY!
AHHH!
THE SUSPECT HAS BEEN POSITIVELY IDENTIFIED.
PANCHO, TAKE HIM AWAY FOR QUESTIONING!

SLAM-A-ROO!
ALRIGHT, MISTER BUSBOY, IF YOU KNOW WHAT'S GOOD FOR YOU,
YOU'LL GIVE US YOUR FULL COOPERATION.
WE JUST WANT THE FACTS, SON.
BUT FIRST, LET'S MAKE SURE YOU'RE COMFY.
JUST RELAX.
HERE ARE SOME CUCUMBER SLICES FOR THOSE TIRED EYES.
WOULD YOU LIKE A PILLOW?
ARE YOU THIRSTY? WOULD YOU LIKE SOME MILK AND COOKIES?
WOULD YOU LIKE ME TO RUB YOUR FEET!?
NO! GROSS. NO!
HEY MAN, LIKE, YOUR GOOD COP/GOOD COP ROUTINE IS FREAKING ME OUT!
HOLD ON A SECOND! I THOUGHT YOU WERE GONNA BE THE BAD COP.
I WAS THE BAD COP LAST TIME. I WAS GONNA LET YOU HAVE A TURN.
BUT YOU'RE SO GOOD AT IT! AND I KNOW HOW MUCH YOU ENJOY IT!
NO NO, YOU'RE THE ONE WITH THE BEST BAD COP ZINGERS!
AH! THANKS, BUDDY.
LOOK, I'M SORRY WE DIDN'T TALK THIS THROUGH FIRST. MY BAD. WE COOL, MAN?
AW, COME HERE, YOU!
YOU KNOW I LOVE YA, YOU OLD HOG!
HOLD IT! WE AREN'T DONE WITH YOU.
I'D BETTER GET BACK TO WORK.

THIS INTERROGATION IS A BUST.
LET'S STEP IT UP A NOTCH!
PANCHO, THE HOT SAUCE!
YEE-HAW! NOW WE'RE TALKING!
POP!
HEY MAN, WHAT ARE YOU DOING?
POP!
IF YOU DON'T TELL US THE LOCATION OF THE MISSING NACHO,
MY PARTNER AND I WILL SUFFER A JALAPEÑO BURNOUT TONGUE-NOOGIE.
MINE IS SPICY HABANERO.
DON'T DO IT, MAN!
THOSE THING ARE REALLY HOT! I'LL TELL YOU WHATEVER YOU WANT!
JUST PUT THE SAUCES DOWN NICE AND SLOW.
HOLD UP, PANCHO! I THINK HE IS ABOUT TO CONFESS!
I'M HOT!
OOPS!
SIZZLE!
AAAAAAA
AAAA
AHHHH!
OOF!

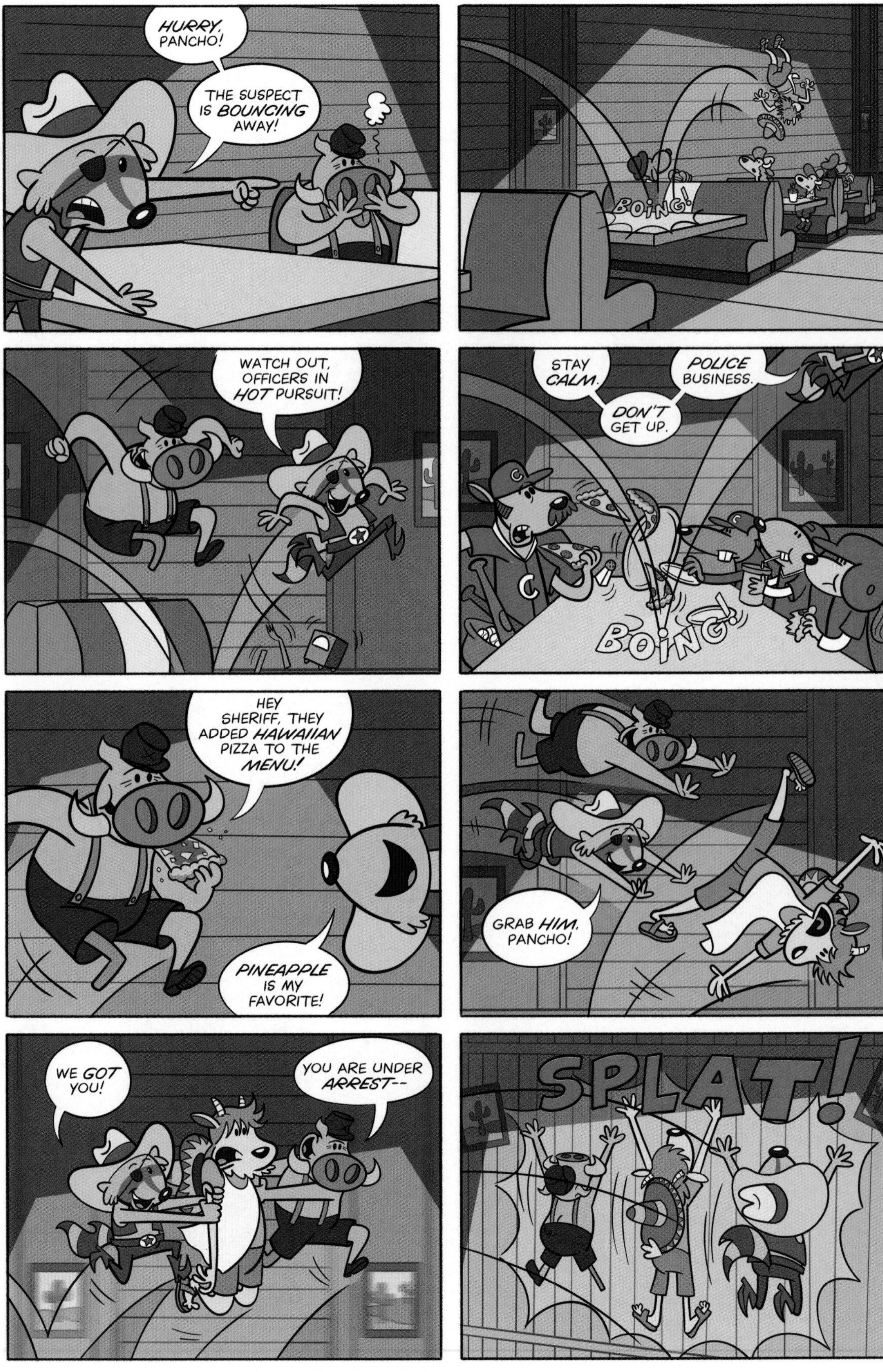
HURRY, PANCHO!
THE SUSPECT IS BOUNCING AWAY!
BOING!
WATCH OUT, OFFICERS IN HOT PURSUIT!
STAY CALM.
DON'T GET UP.
POLICE BUSINESS.
BOING!
HEY SHERIFF, THEY ADDED HAWAIIAN PIZZA TO THE MENU!
PINEAPPLE IS MY FAVORITE!
GRAB HIM, PANCHO!
WE GOT YOU!
YOU ARE UNDER ARREST--
SPLAT!

WELL? DON'T JUST SIT THERE. WHERE IS MY NACHO?
I'M SITTING ON A FORK.
I'M SITTING ON MY CAR KEYS.
I'M SITTING ON AN ANSWER!
I KNOW WHERE THE MISSING NACHO IS!
YOU SEE, MR. MAYOR, YOUR LAST NACHO WAS NEVER STOLEN.
HOLD STILL.
THIS WAS NEVER A NACHO-NAPPING INVESTIGATION AFTER ALL,
BUT A SIMPLE CASE OF LOST AND FOUND!
TA-DA! THERE IT IS!
CRISPY TORTILLAS, SHERIFF!
HOW'D YOU KNOW?
ELEMENTARY, MY DEAR PANCHO.
YOU SEE, ALL THAT BOUNCING AROUND GOT ME THINKING.
WHEN THE MAYOR WENT TO GRAB THE HOT SAUCE,
HE MUST HAVE KICKED THE TABLE UP WITH HIS SHOES.
KICK!
THAT EXPLAINS THE TWO LEFT SHOE PRINTS UNDER THE TABLE.
IT'S NO SECRET THAT THE MAYOR HAS TWO LEFT FEET.
L
L
I CALCULATED THAT AN 850 CALORIE NACHO CHIP TRAVELING AT THE SPEED OF A SNEEZE,
MULTIPLIED BY THE NUMBERS OF TIMES I USED THE WORD NACHO TODAY, DIVIDED BY THE MAYOR'S NEGATIVE ATTITUDE,
850 CALORIES
(10)
EQUALS THE NACHO LANDING ON THE SEAT
AT THE PRECISE MOMENT THE MAYOR SAT DOWN.
SPLAT!

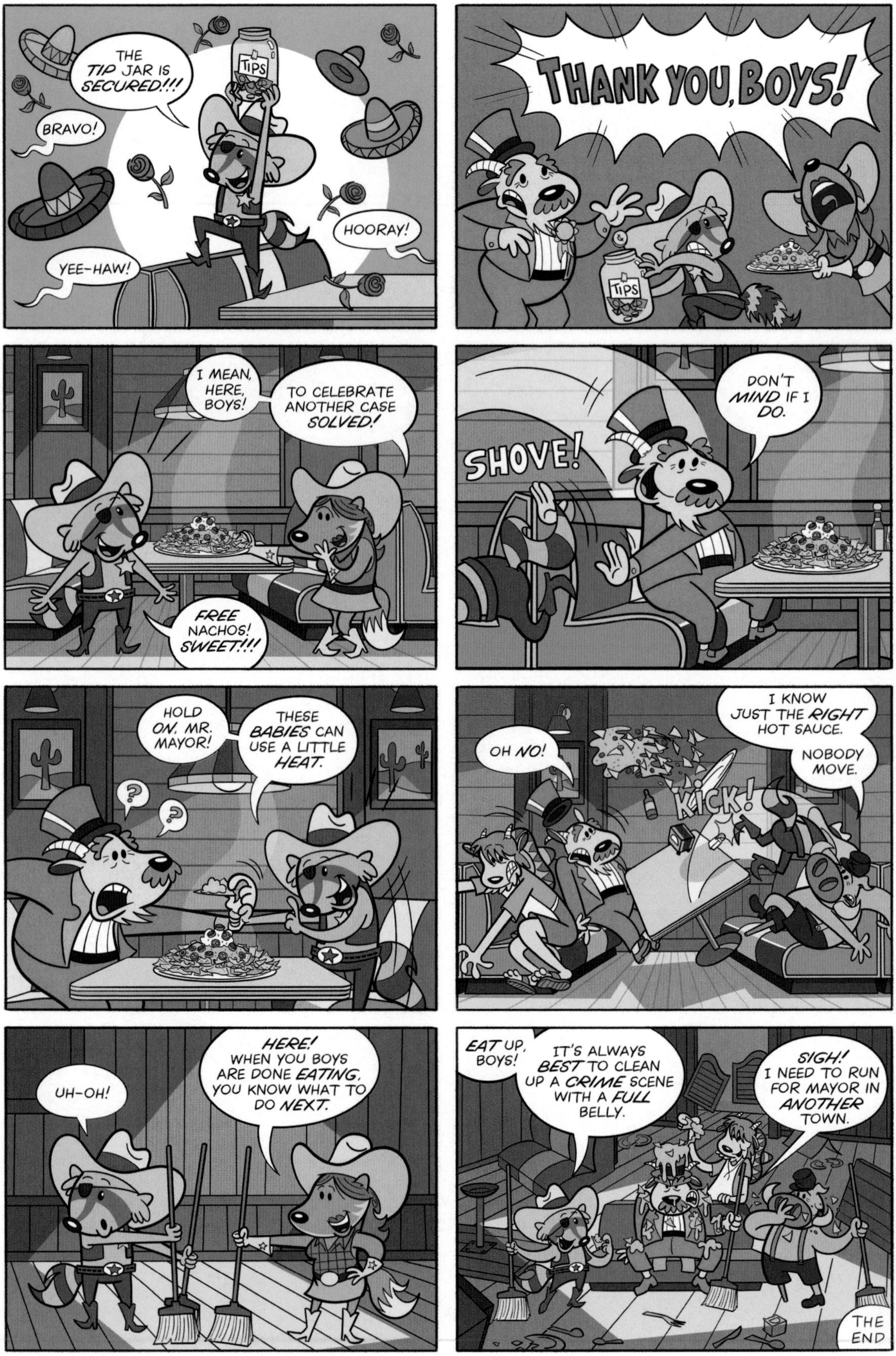
THE TIP JAR IS SECURED!!!
BRAVO!
HOORAY!
YEE-HAW!
THANK YOU, BOYS!
TIPS
I MEAN, HERE, BOYS!
TO CELEBRATE ANOTHER CASE SOLVED!
FREE NACHOS! SWEET!!!
DON'T MIND IF I DO.
SHOVE!
HOLD ON, MR. MAYOR!
THESE BABIES CAN USE A LITTLE HEAT.
?
?
OH NO!
I KNOW JUST THE RIGHT HOT SAUCE.
NOBODY MOVE.
KICK!
UH-OH!
HERE! WHEN YOU BOYS ARE DONE EATING, YOU KNOW WHAT TO DO NEXT.
EAT UP, BOYS!
IT'S ALWAYS BEST TO CLEAN UP A CRIME SCENE WITH A FULL BELLY.
SIGH! I NEED TO RUN FOR MAYOR IN ANOTHER TOWN.
THE END

LUZ AND SATO
IN LOVE CONQUERS ALL
A LITTLE BIT MORE OF CRUSHED FROG'S WARTS SHOULD DO IT.
BOO!
SATO! WOULD YOU CUT THAT OUT?
YOU AREN'T SCARING ANYONE.
REALLY? I THOUGHT THAT BOO SOUNDED PRETTY GOOD.
HEY! WHAT ARE YOU BREWING, LUZ?
I'M MAKING A LOVE POTION PERFUME.
I'LL MAKE A FORTUNE SELLING IT AFTER SCHOOL.
ISN'T LOVE FREE?
AMORE ODORATUS INCANTAMENTUM!
ZAP!
ARGH!!! NOT AGAIN! I KEEP MESSING UP THE RECIPE.
URGH! LOVE STINKS!

OH BOY, ANCIENT SPELLS ARE SO HARD TO READ.
OH, I SEE! I MISTAKENLY USED HAIRS FROM A TOAD INSTEAD OF A FEATHER FROM A DODO BIRD.
BATS! DODO BIRDS HAVE BEEN EXTINCT FOR CENTURIES.
HOLD ON A SECOND, I KNOW WHERE I CAN FIND ONE!
HEH-HEH!
COME ON, SATO, FOLLOW ME!
BOO!
SHRIEK!
MEOW!
OUCH!
OW!
OH MAN! THAT CAT'S NAILS ARE SHARP.
YOU NEVER KNOW WHEN TO QUIT, DO YOU?
HURRY! DON'T JUST STAND THERE. GRAB ON!
HOLD ON TO YOUR HATS!
WAIT! I DON'T HAVE A ...
HAAAT
NEXT STOP, THE MUSEUM OF NATURAL HISTORY!
BOING!

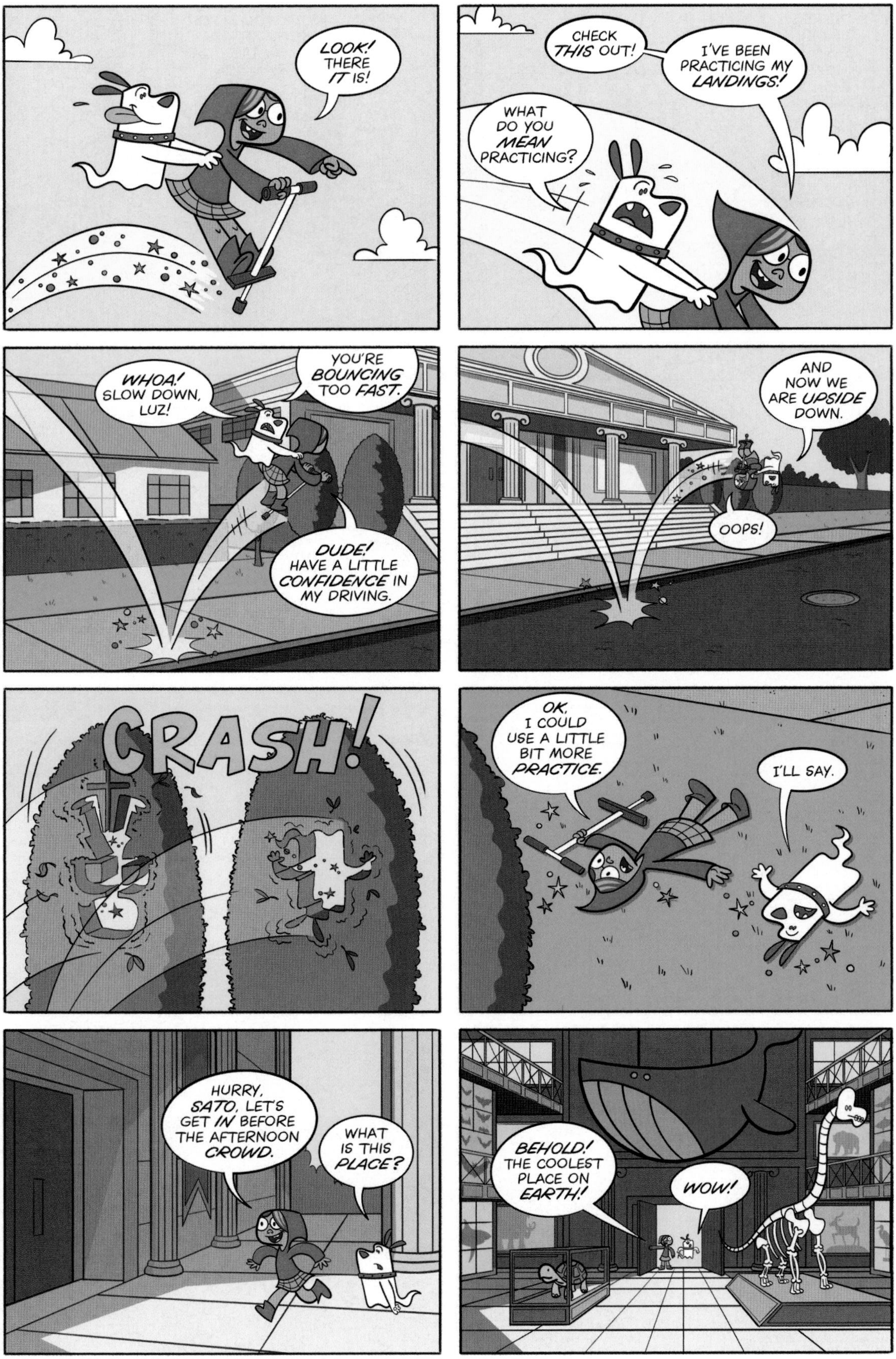
LOOK! THERE IT IS!
CHECK THIS OUT!
I'VE BEEN PRACTICING MY LANDINGS!
WHAT DO YOU MEAN PRACTICING?
WHOA! SLOW DOWN, LUZ!
YOU'RE BOUNCING TOO FAST.
DUDE! HAVE A LITTLE CONFIDENCE IN MY DRIVING.
AND NOW WE ARE UPSIDE DOWN.
OOPS!
CRASH!
OK, I COULD USE A LITTLE BIT MORE PRACTICE.
I'LL SAY.
HURRY, SATO, LET'S GET IN BEFORE THE AFTERNOON CROWD.
WHAT IS THIS PLACE?
BEHOLD! THE COOLEST PLACE ON EARTH!
WOW!

THERE'S THE DODO BIRD, BUT BE QUIET!
THERE IS A GUARD BLOCKING THE EXHIBIT'S ENTRANCE.
DO NOT TOUCH
HEY, I HAVE AN IDEA!
HOW WOULD YOU LIKE A DISGUISE, SATO?
RIDICULAM DISSIMULO RAPIDUS!
NO, THANK YOU!
HA! HA! LOOK AT YOUR MUSTACHE!
MY MUSTACHE IS ITCHY.
SHHH!
STAND BACK! CLEANING CREW COMING THROUGH.
DO NOT TOUCH
GREAT, THE COAST IS CLEAR!
ONE DODO BIRD FEATHER COMING UP!
PLUCKED!
AMORE ODORATUS INCANTAMENTUM!
TZING!
SHABAM! I DID IT!
NOW LET'S RUSH HOME AND BOTTLE IT.
HEY LUZ! ISN'T THAT YOUR "I-WISH-HE-WAS-BOYFRIEND", BOYFRIEND...
...AND HIS MAD SCIENTIST BROTHER?

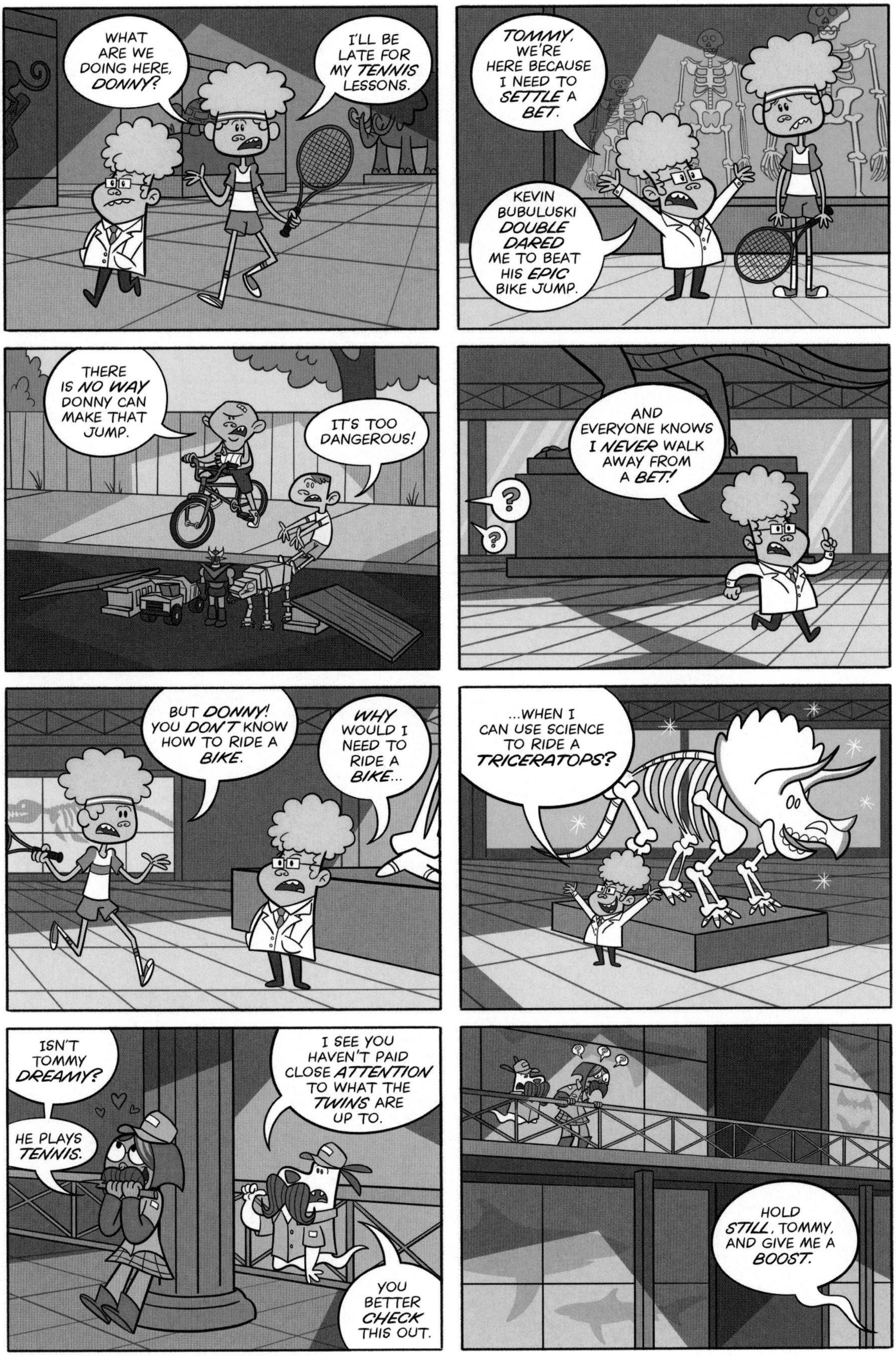

WHAT ARE WE DOING HERE, DONNY?
I'LL BE LATE FOR MY TENNIS LESSONS.
TOMMY, WE'RE HERE BECAUSE I NEED TO SETTLE A BET.
KEVIN BUBULUSKI DOUBLE DARED ME TO BEAT HIS EPIC BIKE JUMP.
THERE IS NO WAY DONNY CAN MAKE THAT JUMP.
IT'S TOO DANGEROUS!
AND EVERYONE KNOWS I NEVER WALK AWAY FROM A BET!
?
?
BUT DONNY! YOU DON'T KNOW HOW TO RIDE A BIKE.
WHY WOULD I NEED TO RIDE A BIKE...
...WHEN I CAN USE SCIENCE TO RIDE A TRICERATOPS?
ISN'T TOMMY DREAMY?
HE PLAYS TENNIS.
I SEE YOU HAVEN'T PAID CLOSE ATTENTION TO WHAT THE TWINS ARE UP TO.
YOU BETTER CHECK THIS OUT.
HOLD STILL, TOMMY, AND GIVE ME A BOOST.

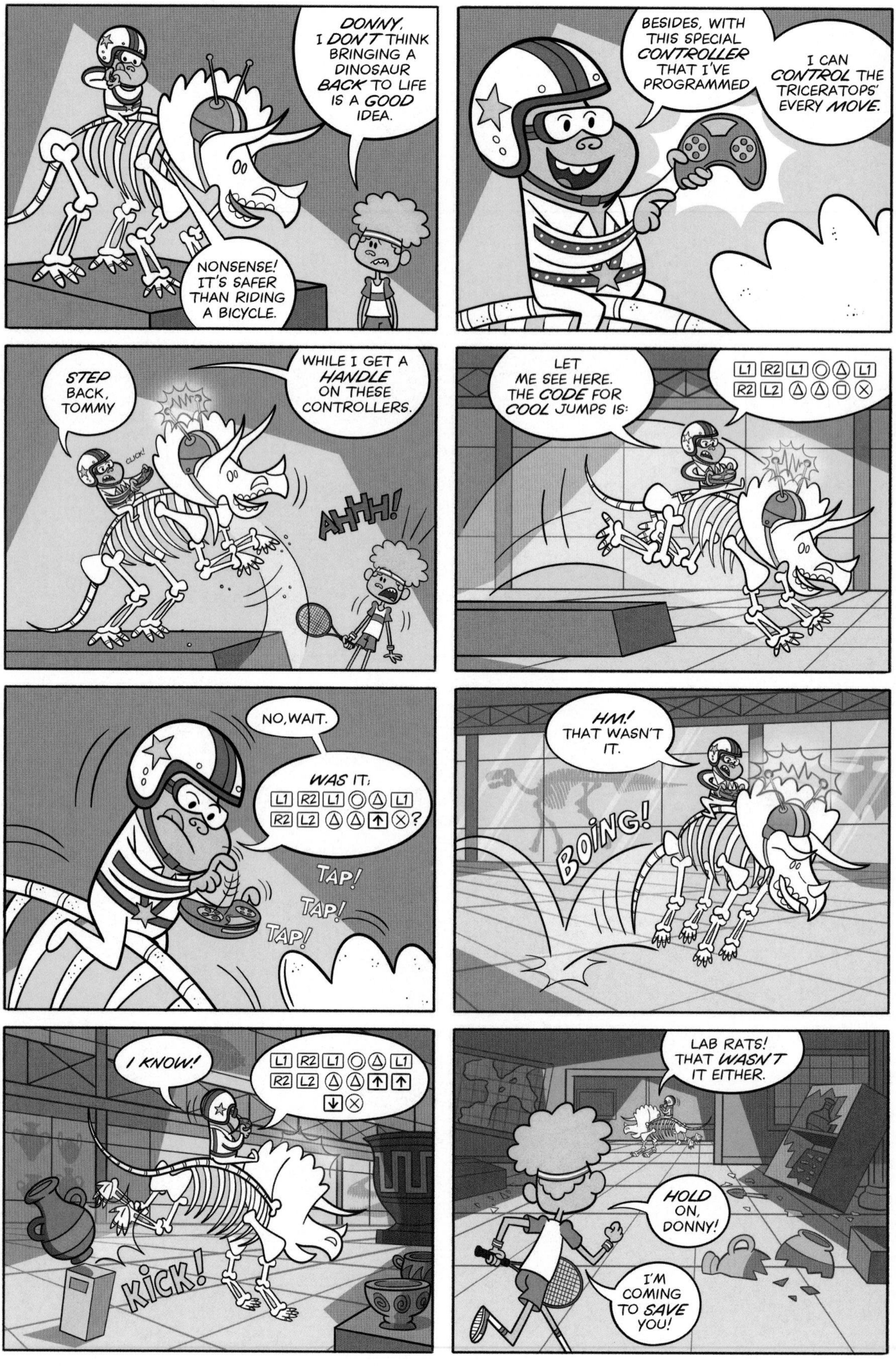
DONNY, I DON'T THINK BRINGING A DINOSAUR BACK TO LIFE IS A GOOD IDEA.
NONSENSE! IT'S SAFER THAN RIDING A BICYCLE.
BESIDES, WITH THIS SPECIAL CONTROLLER THAT I'VE PROGRAMMED
I CAN CONTROL THE TRICERATOPS' EVERY MOVE.
STEP BACK, TOMMY
WHILE I GET A HANDLE ON THESE CONTROLLERS.
CLICK!
AHHH!
LET ME SEE HERE. THE CODE FOR COOL JUMPS IS:
L1 R2 L1 ○ △ L1 R2 L2 △ △ □ ⊗
NO, WAIT.
WAS IT: L1 R2 L1 ○ △ L1 R2 L2 △ △ ↑ ⊗?
TAP!
TAP!
TAP!
HM! THAT WASN'T IT.
BOING!
I KNOW!
L1 R2 L1 ○ △ L1 R2 L2 △ △ ↑ ↑ ↓ ⊗
KICK!
LAB RATS! THAT WASN'T IT EITHER.
HOLD ON, DONNY!
I'M COMING TO SAVE YOU!

YUP! I'M OUT OF HERE.
OH NO!
CRASH!
COME ON, SATO!
WE HAVE TO STOP HIM BEFORE HE DESTROYS THE WHOLE MUSEUM.
OH GREAT!
NOW THE △ BUTTON IS STUCK.
HIT
WAIT UP, BROTHER! I'M COMING!
AAAH!
CRACK!
ZAP!
?
HI, TOMMY!
UH? HI!
YOU KNOW, YOU STILL HAVE A MUSTACHE ON YOUR FACE.
ARGH! WHY DIDN'T YOU TELL ME BEFORE I MADE A FOOL OF MYSELF?
ZAP!
DON'T BLAME ME.
YOU'RE THE ONE WHO LIKES TO PUT MUSTACHES ON EVERYTHING.
WHERE DID I PUT MY FLAT-HEAD SCREWDRIVER?

BEAKERS! THIS BUTTON IS JAMMED IN GOOD.
THERE! I THINK THAT FIXED IT.
SATO, WATCH OUT!
LUZ, WHY DON'T YOU USE YOUR MAGIC TO TURN OFF THE REMOTE CONTROLLER?
BROTHER, BE CAREFUL!
I CAN'T, SATO!
MY MAGIC DOESN'T WORK ON MAD SCIENTIST GADGETS.
WELL, YOU CAN KISS THE PALEOLITHIC STONE TOOLS COLLECTION GOODBYE.
IT'S LIKE A WILD BULL IN A CHINA SHOP OUT THERE.
HOLD ON A SECOND! THAT GIVES ME AN IDEA!
FIRST, WE NEED TO BECOME BULL FIGHTERS.
RIDICULAM DISSIMULO RAPIDUS!
AGAIN WITH THE MUSTACHES!
NOW WITH THIS BULL-FIGHTING CAPE, WE CAN DISTRACT THE BULL.
REALLY? THAT'S YOUR PLAN?
YOU KNOW HE'S NOT AN ACTUAL BULL, RIGHT?
I KNOW, BUT IF I ADD A CRIMSON COLOR SPELL
TO THE LOVE POTION, HE WILL GO BANANAS FOR THE COLOR RED.
COLORO VERMICULUS INCANTAMENTUM!

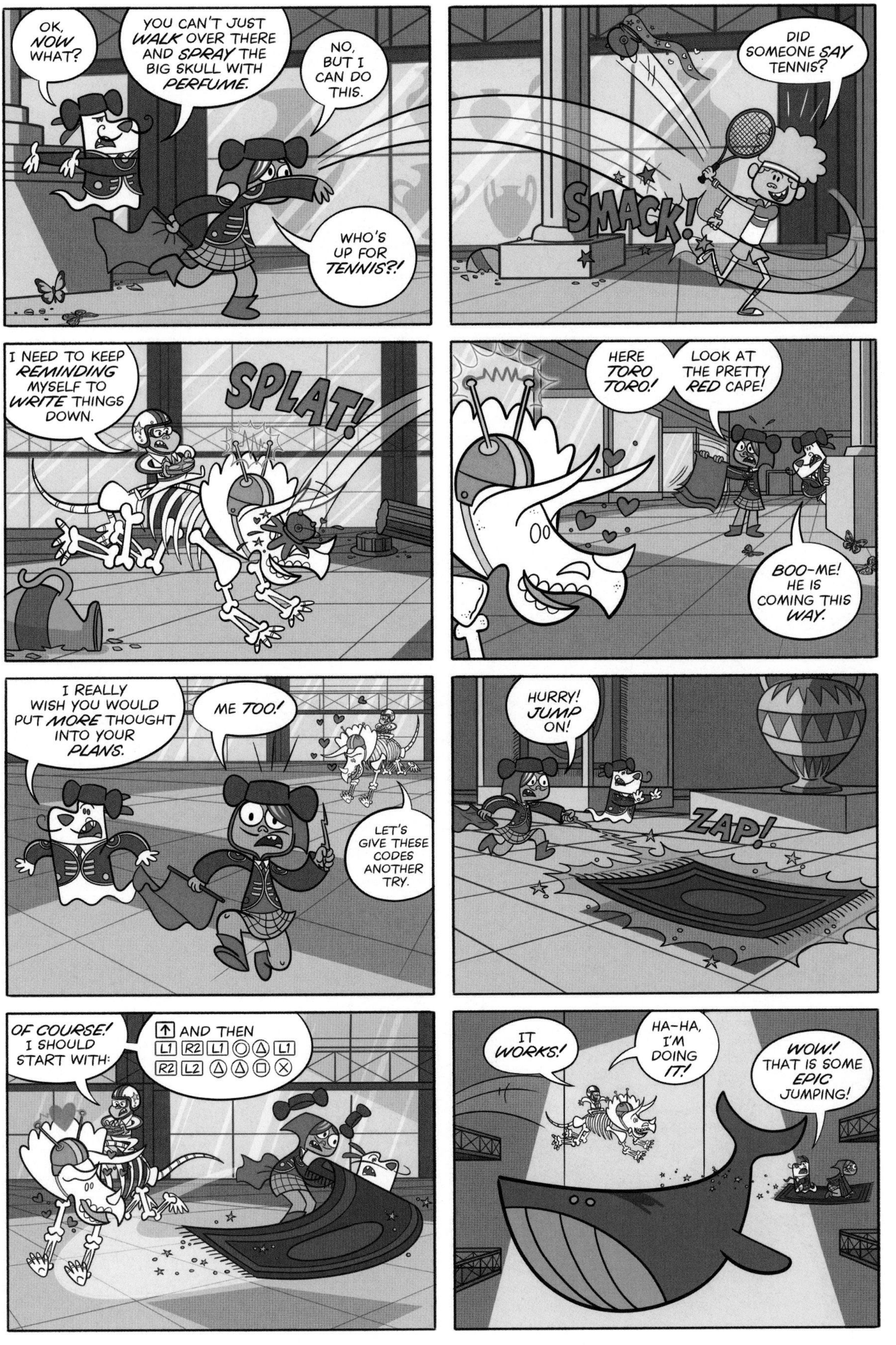
OK, NOW WHAT?
YOU CAN'T JUST WALK OVER THERE AND SPRAY THE BIG SKULL WITH PERFUME.
NO, BUT I CAN DO THIS.
WHO'S UP FOR TENNIS?!
DID SOMEONE SAY TENNIS?
SMACK!
I NEED TO KEEP REMINDING MYSELF TO WRITE THINGS DOWN.
SPLAT!
HERE TORO TORO!
LOOK AT THE PRETTY RED CAPE!
BOO-ME! HE IS COMING THIS WAY.
I REALLY WISH YOU WOULD PUT MORE THOUGHT INTO YOUR PLANS.
ME TOO!
LET'S GIVE THESE CODES ANOTHER TRY.
HURRY! JUMP ON!
ZAP!
OF COURSE! I SHOULD START WITH:
↑ AND THEN L1 R2 L1 ○ △ L1 R2 L2 △ △ □ ✕
IT WORKS!
HA-HA, I'M DOING IT!
WOW! THAT IS SOME EPIC JUMPING!

HE'S CATCHING UP TO US FAST.
UH! I WOULDN'T WORRY TOO MUCH ABOUT IT.
JUMP!
WHOA, HORSEY! SLOW DOWN!
CRASH!
UMPH! BACK TO THE DRAWING BOARD.
PLEASE TELL ME SOMEONE SAW ME MAKE THAT AWESOME JUMP?
Z Z Z
EARLY MAN
HUFF! I'M GLAD THAT'S OVER.
I BETTER CALL MY MOM TO PICK US UP.
HI, TOMMY!
OH! HI, LUZ.
I REALLY LIKE WHAT YOU DID TO YOUR MUSTACHE.
SATO! WHY DIDN'T YOU WARN ME?
WHY ARE YOU COMPLAINING?
HE FINALLY NOTICED YOU.
THE END

LUZ AND SATO
GOOD JOB, SISTERS!
WITH THIS EVER-LASTING PEPPERMINT FRESH BREATH POTION, WE ARE GETTING AN A+ THIS SEMESTER FOR SURE!
Witch Coven 101
Wood Shop 101
IT TASTES GREAT!
SIP!
SATO!
HEY LADIES! WHAT ABOUT ADDING MORE SPICES TO THIS BATH? IT'S GREAT AT GETTING RID OF MY FLEAS.
AHHH!
GROSS!
SATO, YOU ARE THE WORST!
WHEN I CATCH YOU, I'M GOING TO PUT A CURSE ON YOU!
DON'T BOTHER, LUZ! YOUR POTION ALREADY CURSED ME WITH A MAGICAL RASH!
SCRATCH!
SCRATCH!
SCRATCH!
THE END

HIP AND POPO
LOOK, HIP!
THAT'S THE ELUSIVE GIANT WHIPLASH TOAD, KNOWN FOR ITS INCREDIBLY FAST-SHOOTING TONGUE.
YUM!
IT SURE LOOKS HUNGRY.
BUZZ
WIP!
THEY'RE ALSO KNOWN FOR THEIR TERRIBLE AIM.
HAHA! I'LL SAY.
TEE-HEE!
SIGH!
THE END

LUNA DESTINY
CHECK THIS OUT, BARN! WHY ROAST A PUNY MARSHMALLOW, WHEN I JUST ENLARGED ONE BY 500% WITH THE GROW-A-LOT 9000 OVEN?
OH NO, LUNA!
KEEP THAT THING AWAY!
A MARSHMALLOW THAT'S 500% BIGGER IS...
KA-WOOSH!
SPLAT!
OOPS!
... IS ALSO 500% MORE COMBUSTIBLE!
SPLAT!
SPLAT!
THE END

SHERIFF RATTATAN AND DEPUTY PANCHO
THERE HE IS!
THANK GOODNESS WE FOUND YOU, MR. MAYOR!
WE WERE STUMPED TRYING TO SOLVE THE LAST RIDDLE YOUR KIDNAPPERS LEFT US TO FIND YOU.
IT'S ABOUT TIME YOU GUYS SHOWED UP TO RESCUE ME!
LISTEN CAREFULLY TO THESE CLUES:
WHAT SNEEZES IN PAIRS AND ALWAYS ARRIVES ON TIME?
EASY-PEASY!
THAT WOULD BE A CHOO-CHOO TRAIN.
THE 12:15 EXPRESS TO LA ROCA, TO BE PRECISE.
OF COURSE!
COME ON, PANCHO! LET'S GO AND FIND MORE FUN RIDDLES TO SOLVE!
MAN, RIDDLES ARE EASY WHEN SOMEONE ELSE KNOWS THE ANSWER!
WHY DO I BOTHER WITH THEM?
THOSE TWO ARE ALWAYS A PUZZLE TO ME.
CHOO-CHOO!
THE END

POP!
CRASH!
BROOM
WAAAH!!!
BROOM
SHRIEK!
ZAP
AHRRRR!
BEEP!
BEEP!
BEEP!
BEEP!
BEEP!
BEEP!
BEEP!
ZOOM!
BUZZZ
GRRRR!
PUFF!
HA-HA!
WHOOSH!
SPLAT!
SNIP!
DROP
HEH-HEH!
SIP!
RUMLE!
SHOOSH!
FWOOSH!
GRRR!!
HAR-HA!
SPLAT!
THWAP!
BOOM!
SLAP!
BOING!
ZOOM!
SLAM!
ZZZING!!!
MAN, TALKING IN SOUND EFFECTS IS A LOT OF FUN!
BEEP YEAH!
THE END

Hiccups
Hiccups
Fun Stories
#0
$3.99
Hiccups
Fun Stories
E
By Miguel Martinez Joffre
RIDICULAM COMICUS LIBER!
SO THAT'S HOW COMIC BOOKS ARE MADE!
THE END

COME ON HIP, LET'S HELP THE QUEEN BRING THIS JUICY PINEAPPLE TO HER BABIES.
WHAT ARE WE WAITING FOR? LET'S GO!
WHO KNEW SO MANY BABIES EATING AT ONCE WOULD BE THIS LOUD?
THEY ARE LOUD, BUT SO CUTE!
MUNCH! MUNCH! MUNCH! MUNCH! MUNCH! MUNCH! MUNCH!
YUM! YUM! YUM!
THE END

GOOD KICK, LUNA!
PASS IT, POPO!
I GOT THIS!
GOAL!
OH!
WAIT A MINUTE, I THOUGHT YOU WERE ON MY TEAM!
NO WAY, TENNIS IS MY GAME!
ZAP!
THE END

SKETCH PAGE

SKETCH PAGE

SKETCH PAGE

SKETCH PAGE

SKETCH PAGE

SKETCH PAGE

SKETCH PAGE

SKETCH PAGE

Sketch Page

SKETCH PAGE

SKETCH PAGE

SKETCH PAGE